Poptropica

PENCIL WARRIOR

Poptropica

An Imprint of Penguin Group (USA) Inc.

cover designed by Ching Chan
with illustrations by The Artifact Group

POPTROPICA
Published by the Penguin Group
Penguin Group (USA) Inc., 375 Hudson Street,
New York, New York 10014, USA
Penguin Group (Canada), 90 Eglinton Avenue East, Suite 700, Toronto,
Ontario M4P 2Y3, Canada (a division of Pearson Penguin Canada Inc.)
Penguin Books Ltd, 80 Strand, London WC2R 0RL, England
Penguin Ireland, 25 St Stephen's Green, Dublin 2,
Ireland (a division of Penguin Books Ltd)
Penguin Group (Australia), 707 Collins Street, Melbourne, Victoria
3008, Australia (a division of Pearson Australia Group Pty Ltd)
Penguin Books India Pvt Ltd, 11 Community Centre,
Panchsheel Park, New Delhi—110 017, India
Penguin Group (NZ), 67 Apollo Drive, Rosedale, Auckland 0632,
New Zealand (a division of Pearson New Zealand Ltd)
Penguin Books, Rosebank Office Park, 181 Jan Smuts
Avenue, Parktown North 2193, South Africa
Penguin China, B7 Jaiming Center, 27 East Third Ring Road
North, Chaoyang District, Beijing 100020, China

Penguin Books Ltd, Registered Offices: 80 Strand, London WC2R 0RL, England

ISBN 978-0-448-46230-1   10 9 8 7 6 5 4 3 2 1

ALWAYS LEARNING   **PEARSON**

Arthur Eraser—aka The Eraser, or Art Eraser to his one friend (who's imaginary)—is a notorious supervillain who has just been spotted in Poptropica. He is armed with a superpowered pencil that can erase anything it touches. Be careful; he is extremely dangerous.

HAHAHAHAHA! POWERLESS POPTROPICANS, EVERYTHING YOU HOLD DEAR WILL SOON BE MINE. WITH MY SUPER ERASER AND MY GENIUS BRAIN, I WILL STEAL ALL OF POPTROPICA FOR MYSELF. SOON I WILL HAVE AN ISLAND OF MY OWN: EVIL ERASER ISLAND. AND IT WILL BE FILLED WITH ALL YOUR FAVORITE THINGS, BUT IT WILL BE ONLY FOR ME. I WILL OWN IT ALL! AND YOU WILL HAVE NOTHING!

SO, DO YOU THINK YOU CAN STOP ME WITH YOUR FEEBLE PENCIL THAT'S NOWHERE NEAR AS SUPER AS MINE? YOU MAKE ME LAUGH. HAHAHAHAHA! GO ON—TRY TO CATCH ME IF YOU CAN. I DARE YOU. MWAHAHAHAHA!

SKULLDUGGERY
ISLAND

The riffraff down at the Pirate Outpost are telling a crazy story about a vandal with a magic pencil! The last thing I need is for those ne'er-do-wells to cause a ruckus. Can you investigate, and help them put back what they've lost?

We've gotten another report of the mysterious vandal from Golden Harbor. The bank has been erased—and our town's treasury along with it! Make haste and restore our riches before our creditors find out.

This is the last straw. Someone has erased the shipbuilder's den in Dragon Cove, and no one is going to be able to sail the seas without it. Who is this dastardly villain? He makes Captain Crawfish look like a tadpole!

 I've never seen anything like it! Some deity I've never seen before appeared out of nowhere and erased all the statues from my father's throne room. If my father sees this, he'll be furious!

A squat little man with some kind of magic wand just ran through here and stole one of our sacred statues. The Poptropolis Games will be ruined. More importantly, I'll be a laughingstock! Help celebrate our ancient champions by drawing in the statue.

Before the eternal flame can be lit and tribal representatives rise to compete for a chance to become the next champion, someone must clean up Main Street. It's a mess! I'm embarrassed to be seen there.

Before you leave Poptropolis, there is just one more statue that needs to be fixed. If you're planning to take a ship to wherever it is you're going, you may want to patch that up, too...

110

120

130

140

SUPER POWER ISLAND

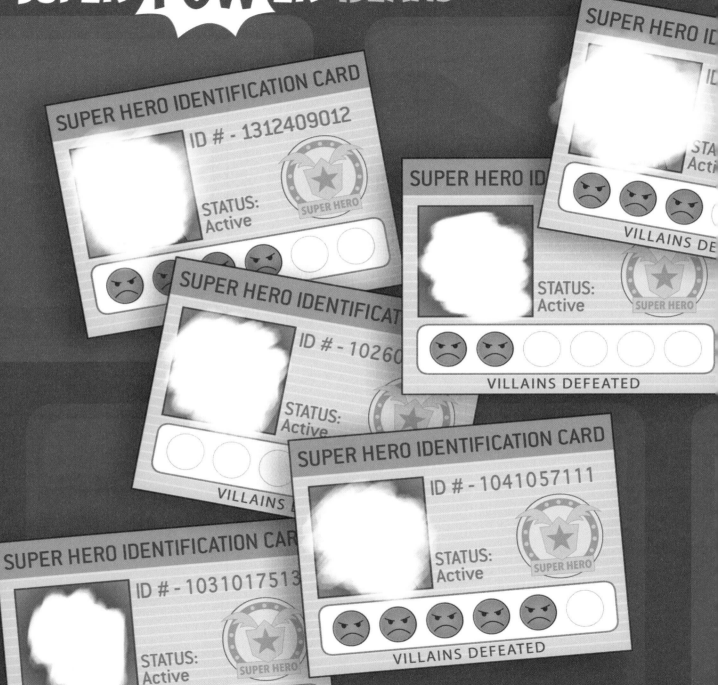

SUPER HERO IDENTIFICATION CARD

ID # - 1312409012

STATUS: Active

SUPER HERO ID

STATUS: Active

VILLAINS DE

VILLAINS DEFEATED

SUPER HERO IDENTIFICAT

ID # - 10260

STATUS: Active

VILLAINS

SUPER HERO IDENTIFICATION CARD

ID # - 1041057111

STATUS: Active

SUPER HERO

VILLAINS DEFEATED

SUPER HERO IDENTIFICATION CAR

ID # - 1031017513

STATUS: Active

SUPER HERO

VILLAINS DEFEATED

SUPER HERO IDENTIFICATION CARD

ID # - 2101351703

STATUS: Active

SUPER HERO IDENTIFICATION CARD

ID # - 1026020971

STATUS: Active

VILLAINS DEFEATED

IFICATION CARD

1418411813

SUPER HERO

ED

SUPER HERO IDENTIFICATION CARD

ID # - 1024997011

STATUS: Active

SUPER HERO

VILLAINS DEF

SUPER HERO

ID # - 1536120873

STATUS: Active

SUPER HERO

VILLAINS DEFEATED

SUPER HERO IDENTIFICATION CARD

ID # - 2146358101

STATUS: Active

SUPER HERO

VILLAINS DEFEATED

It looks like Super Power Island has a new supervillain on the streets. We've got a case of stolen identities! No superhero can fight crime without a valid ID. Help keep Super Power Island safe from evildoers by giving each hero back their identity.

There has been a break-in at the bank! It's up to you to suit up and take down this devious villain by replacing what is missing. Then Super Power Island will be safe...for now.

24 CARROT ISLAND

As if times weren't hard enough here on 24 Carrot Island, it appears that someone has been messing with our sign. We may not be able to get our carrots back, but you can at least help replace the bunny on this historic landmark.

Deep in his lair, Dr. Hare is taking all of our carrots and using them for rocket fuel. However, Dr. Hare isn't able to escape into space just yet since something was stolen from his rocket. Can you spot the missing piece and make the needed repairs? Then he'll be out of our *hare* for good. Get it?

Our town relies on the factory to produce our beloved carrots, but someone stripped the machinery! Without the right pieces in place, the assembly line isn't going to work. Replace the missing parts and help with the carrot production.

MASTER ENGINE

Someone done messed with Dos Cactos! No one's goin' to be playing slapjack or entering the shootin' contest anytime soon. That gets me hotter than a Texas rattlesnake in July. Once you draw the signs back in, I'm sure business will be boomin' again in Dos Cactos.

The Grande Gang is the least of McGready's worries. Help replace all the valuable tokens that have been erased, especially McGready's most-prized possessions: his portraits of himself.

Arthur Eraser thinks he can run wild in these parts. Well, not on my watch. I'm headin' into the desert to look for him. In the meantime, some of Dusty Gulch's buildings could use a good ole fixer-upper, Deputy.

Twisted Thicket

The enchanted forest has been disrupted. Certain parts of the sacred tree have vanished. I know you have a good heart and will help restore the source of our forest's magic. Hurry, before we are turned into stone!

The noble rock trolls are the strongest creatures in my realm. What dark power could have whisked them away? Please replace the trolls on their hill, and those bones that they hold so dear.

The entrance to the sacred tree, and my throne room, has been sealed by a magical power. My dryad informants tell me that someone wielding an enchanted pencil came through this way. Can you draw in what's missing from the forest? I would be forever grateful.

Error 437: Missing pieces at production zone. Need to power steam engine. Restart production. Stop no-good thief!

Parts missing from buildings on Main Street like Zack missing
from Sprocket. Please help Sprocket. Maybe new Main Street
will bring everyone back.

Sully's Garage missing tools, chalkboard checklist, and Mech. Strange laughing person seen leaving the scene. Sprocket needs your help to replace lost parts.

It looks like I'm not the only one causing trouble around here. Someone has been messing around on the dock. Some super-duper-secret spy technology is missing. Please replace the satellite dish and whatever else you find missing.

B.A.D

Without the Headquarters and the Hair Club, the island will no longer be able to train its top agents. Not that it matters to me, but I'm sure the Secretary of the agency would be pleased if you were to draw back in the island's missing components.

The main control center has vanished! If only I had thought of that first... It's up to you, as one of the new top agents, to restore Headquarters to normalcy.

SHRINK RAY ISLAND

Someone has been in my room and tampering with my things. If only I could catch them and use the shrink ray on them! Draw my telescope, doll, and gadgets back into my room for me. I'll look for the thief.

The kitchen is actually looking cleaner than usual...too clean. I think some items have been erased from the kitchen. Please draw in the toaster, cleaning supplies, and fridge art and magnets—before my parents find out.

CAFFEINE

Not only is Mr. Silva after me and my gadgets, but someone is after Mr. Silva and *his* gadgets! Someone has stolen the items from his desk. The quicker you draw them back in, the quicker you can come and rescue me from Mr. Silva's lair. I have to get to the science fair!

YOUR GUTS AND STUFF